D0592848

The Shoes of Salvation

you know who you are

HarperCollins*Entertainment*
An Imprint of HarperCollins*Publishers*
77–85 Fulham Palace Road,
Hammersmith, London W6 8JB

www.harpercollins.co.uk

Published by HarperCollins*Entertainment* 2004
1 3 5 7 9 8 6 4 2

The Author asserts the moral right to
be identified as the author of this work

A catalogue record for this book
is available from the British Library

ISBN 0 00 717845 X

Printed by Proost

The SHOES of SALVATION

There was once a
LADY.

Even though the lady
was not RICH, she was
not POOR either.

And even though she was beset by the small NUISANCES of everyday life, she was CONTENT enough.

But the lady could not help feeling that there was something MISSING.

There was a hollowness, an EMPTINESS in her that needed to be FILLED.

She knew that out there, SOMEWHERE, was Something that could CHANGE her life completely.

Make her WHOLE.
Give her MEANING.

Perhaps
a MAN...

... a JOURNEY...

... a spiritual
AWAKENING...

... a holy and
mysterious
CALLING...

and then she saw
THE BEAUTIFUL
SHOES
and she knew that
they were all she needed.

"Come to us, lady," said
the shoes, "and we will
make you BEAUTIFUL too.

"We alone can make you
blossom and flourish into
a glorious and whole and
COMPLETE Human Being."

"But you are so EXPENSIVE," said the lady. "I cannot possibly afford you."

"Look at our beautiful STRAPS," said the shoes. "Look at our wonderful SHINY leather. Look at the turn of our heels and the shape of our toes.

"Do you think we should be cheaper? Do you think everyone should be able to **AFFORD** the happiness, the pleasure, the **ECSTASY** that we can offer?"

"You are right," said the lady. "I am sorry that I ever doubted you. Please FORGIVE me."

So the lady gave the shopkeeper ALL the MONEY she had and she walked away with the BEAUTIFUL shoes.

When the lady got home,
she tried on the shoes.
Instantly, they began to
PINCH and to HURT
the lady's feet terribly.

"Oh, shoes," said the lady,
"I thought you would bring
me ECSTASY, but all I
can feel is PAIN!"

"Oh, lady," said the shoes, "the pain we GIVE you is simply to remind you of our PRESENCE. Do you not want it to be constantly in your mind that we are here on your feet, making you WONDERFUL, making you GLORIOUS, causing you to shine and to DAZZLE?"

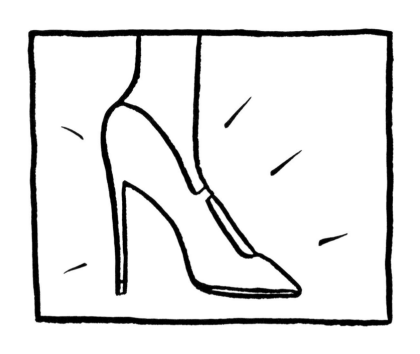

"You are right again," said the lady. "Thank you, shoes."

That evening, the lady wore the BEAUTIFUL shoes to a cocktail party.

Despite the AGONY and the terrible price of the shoes, the lady knew that she felt better than any man or journey or holy and MYSTERIOUS calling could possibly ever make her feel.

For the first time in her life, the lady felt COMPLETE.

And the lady knew what she had INSTINCTIVELY known all along.

That sometimes, only GLORIOUS SHOES can SAVE you.

THE END